THE EXTRAORDINARY FILES

Mind Games

Paul Blum

RISING ★ STARS

'The truth is inside us.
It is the only place where it can hide.'

nasen

nasen
Helping Everyone Achieve

NASEN House, 4/5 Amber Business Village, Amb
Amington, Tamworth, Staffordshire B77 4RP

Rising Stars UK Ltd.
22 Grafton Street, London W1S 4EX
www.risingstars-uk.com

Text © Rising Stars UK Ltd.
The right of Paul Blum to be identified as the author of this work has
been asserted by him in accordance with the Copyright, Design and
Patents Act 1988.

Published 2007

Cover design: Button plc
Illustrator: Aleksandar Sotiroski
Text design and typesetting: pentacor**big**
Publisher: Gill Budgell
Editor: Maoliosa Kelly
Editorial consultants: Lorraine Petersen and Cliff Moon

British Library Cataloguing in Publication Data.
A CIP record for this book is available from the British Library.

ISBN: 978-1-84680-254-6

Printed by Craft Print International Limited, Singapore

CHAPTER ONE

MI5 Headquarters, Vauxhall, London

Agent Laura Turnbull and Agent Robert Parker were British Secret Service Agents. They worked for MI5.

Agent Turnbull had been having headaches. She had also been having strange dreams. Agent Parker had been worried about her for months.

"I told Commander Watson about my headaches and he said I must see an MI5 doctor at the secret research lab this afternoon," said Turnbull.

Parker groaned and put his head in his hands. "Laura, why are you going to see an MI5 doctor? I told you they can't be trusted."

4

"Agent Parker, what's wrong with you? You really have it in for MI5. We are all working on the same side you know!" she said.

He wished he could tell her what
he knew. He wished he could tell her
about the strange metal implant
in her skull, the one he had seen
on the X-ray. He was sure that
Agent Turnbull had had more than
just an operation on her broken
foot that night in the hospital a year
ago. He was sure that Commander
Watson was behind it but he had
no proof, yet.

"I'll come with you," he said.

"Okay, partner," she replied.

They went to the medical research lab.
Commander Watson was there, and two agents
they didn't know. The two agents led Turnbull away.
Parker tried to follow them but Commander Watson
stopped him.

"Agent Parker, don't worry. Your partner is in safe
hands," said Commander Watson.

Parker decided to confront Watson. "What is the
metal object you had put into her head?" he asked.

Commander Watson didn't look surprised.
"Turnbull is a very special agent," he said. "She has
psychic powers. We're interested in her mind."

"And I'm interested in her safety. She doesn't even
know about the implant!" snapped Parker.

"I'll tell her everything she needs to know,"
said Commander Watson. "For now, she's being
put on a special mission. You should go home."

The two agents led Parker away.

"Don't forget, I'm watching everything you do,"
he shouted.

"And *we* are watching everything *you* do, Parker,"
said Watson quietly as he smiled to himself.

CHAPTER TWO

It was a dark and silent night. Parker shone his torch along the wall of the research lab.

Two minutes later, he had climbed in through a small window.

Parker tiptoed down a dark corridor towards a room
with a light on. As soon as he opened the door, he saw
Turnbull sitting in a chair with a strange helmet on
her head. On the wall behind her there was a big
screen. It was like being in a cinema and a film was
just beginning.

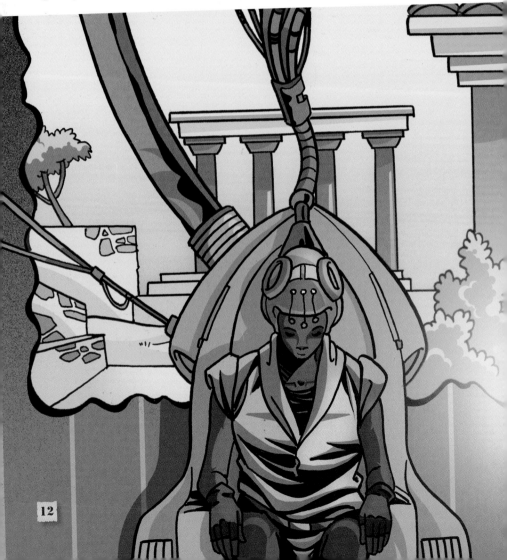

"Agent Parker, you're just in time. The film you are starring in is about to start," said a strange voice.

"What are you talking about?" shouted Parker.

Two men pushed him into a chair and strapped his hands and legs down. He tried to stop them pushing a helmet over his head. Then he blacked out.

When he woke, Turnbull was holding his hand.

"Where am I?" he asked.

"Welcome to the world of Ancient Crete," she said. "We are in my dream world. We are having a real-life, 3D adventure in my mind. If you don't believe me, here is the script," she said.

They read the first page together. "You are in Crete in 1450 BC. You are about to meet King Minos. He needs help. But first you will meet his daughter."

14

They walked down the dusty road towards a palace on top of a big, white hill.

"I'm really hot," said Parker. "Maybe we could get something to drink in here?"

At that moment, a young woman came out of the palace.

"Welcome travellers. I have been expecting you. I am Princess Alison," she said. She pointed to the palace. "You look hot and tired. Come in and refresh yourselves."

Inside the palace, there was a lovely garden. It was cool and shady, with fountains everywhere. The servants gave them cold drinks.

"Now I will tell you my story," she said.

"Are you King Minos' daughter?" asked Turnbull.

"I am David Minos' daughter, actually. He was the greatest scientist to work for MI5, until the experiment."

"What experiment?" Parker asked.

"My father discovered a drug that could unlock
the secrets of the mind. MI5 wanted him to test the
drug in any way he could. My father took a big risk.
He tested the drug on his own family.

On the night of the experiment, a stranger came to
our house and warned my father that he would be
cursed if he messed with nature. But my father didn't
listen to the warnings. He wanted to know what
would happen if he gave us the drug."

"And what did happen?" Turnbull asked.

"We found ourselves here. My brother Roger had turned into a monster, half man and half bull. He had become the Minotaur of the Greek Myths," she said sadly. "He lives in a maze of tunnels under the palace. The curse will be lifted when he is dead."

"Oh no, let me guess," groaned Parker. "You want *us* to kill the Minotaur?"

Alison nodded. "Your partner has special powers. Her mind is so powerful that she can succeed where many others have failed," said Alison.

"But if we kill the Minotaur, we'll also kill your brother," said Turnbull gently.

Alison sighed. "My brother is already dead. That thing down in the maze of tunnels under the palace is not human. By killing it you will put it out of its misery and end this nightmare for us all!"

Turnbull pulled out her sword. It gleamed in the sun. "I'll do the best I can," she said.

"Hang on a minute, Laura," said Parker. "I broke into the lab to keep you safe. This is too dangerous. Let's go home now, before it's too late!"

Turnbull smiled at him. "Robert, you seem to have forgotten that we are actors in a film and we cannot leave before it ends."

Parker put his head in his hands and groaned.

CHAPTER THREE

Alison took them to the maze of tunnels.

"This is where the Minotaur lives," she said.
"The maze of tunnels is like a prison. The Minotaur cannot find its way out."

Parker shivered. "Sounds like a good idea to me.
Just let sleeping dogs lie!"

Alison hugged Agent Turnbull and wished her good luck. "Is there any point taking your friend?" she asked, looking at Parker, who was pale and shaking.

Turnbull nodded. "He's my partner
and we always stick together."

23

They walked through the tunnels for hours.

"Maybe we won't find it," said Parker, hopefully.

"We're getting closer," Turnbull answered, sniffing the air. "I can smell it."

24

Suddenly they heard the sound of snorting and stamping. Something was charging down a tunnel very near to them.

"Hide!" Turnbull commanded.

25

They hid in the shadows. A few seconds later,
the Minotaur passed them. It was a terrible sight.
The lower half of its body had the legs of a man, but
with hooves for feet. Where a human face should
have been, there was the massive head of a bull.
It shook its head and banged its horns against the
wall. White foam was coming from its nostrils.

It paused, then it ran off into the darkness.

"That was a lucky escape," said Parker.

"We must follow it," said Turnbull.

"Are you mad? Did you see that thing? It's time to dream up our escape, before it's too late," said Parker.

Turnbull didn't listen to him. She ran on down the tunnel. Parker followed her but the Minotaur was waiting for them around the next corner. Turnbull tried to use her sword, but with one shake of its huge head, the Minotaur knocked it out of her hand. By the time Parker had got his sword out, the creature had taken Turnbull away, into the darkness.

Parker carried on down the tunnel. He called out
Laura's name but there was no answer.

"This 3D dream is turning into a real-life nightmare,"
he whispered to himself.

He sat down, feeling lost. Turnbull had the map,
compass and script to the film.

He hadn't a clue how to give this film a happy ending.
Suddenly, he felt very tired.

It was then that the stranger sat down beside him.

"Agent Parker," he said. "Would you like some help?"

"I'm interested in any ideas anyone has to get me out of this mess," Parker said. "Who are you, anyway?"

The stranger ignored his question and took a mirror out of his pocket.

"My mirror shows you two futures," he said. "If you come with me, we can get help to kill the Minotaur. If you stay here, you and Agent Turnbull will both die horrible deaths," he said. "Which future do you choose?"

Parker thought for a while, then he said, "If I go with you to get help, then Agent Turnbull will be alone down here with the Minotaur and in that time she

could be killed. I can't leave my partner alone in this terrible place, even to get help."

"Then you and your partner are doomed!" said the stranger.
"You will both die horrible deaths in this dark tunnel. You have made your choice!"

Then he disappeared as suddenly as he had appeared.

Agent Parker carried on until he came to a wider tunnel. He saw a flaming torch at the end of it. He had found the Minotaur's cave. This time he drew his sword in plenty of time to fight.

A strange sight met his eyes. Turnbull was sitting on the floor with her eyes closed. Her hands were tied up. The Minotaur was putting food and drink in front of her as if it was trying to be friendly.

The food didn't look very nice. It was just a pile
of old bones that Turnbull pushed away with her foot.
Suddenly, the Minotaur swung round angrily. It could
hear every tiny sound and knew someone was there.
Parker saw it had red eyes and flaring nostrils. It roared
like an angry bull, foam dribbling from its mouth.

"Robert, is that you?" Turnbull screamed.
"Stay away from me. Save your own life!"

But the Minotaur could smell Parker. Parker was so frightened he froze on the spot. The Minotaur galloped towards him. Parker could smell its sweat. Parker closed his eyes and stabbed out in front of him over and over again.

The Minotaur screamed in pain. It tried to attack Parker but it was too weak. Suddenly, it fell to the floor.

As Parker and Turnbull looked on in horror, the Minotaur's dead body changed back into Roger, Alison's brother.

CHAPTER FOUR

Turnbull and Parker went back to the palace to find King Minos. Parker recognised him from the labs at MI5, but he looked thinner and sadder now.

Alison told him of the Minotaur's death.

"At least Roger can be at peace now," he sighed.

Parker told them about the stranger he had met and the two choices he had been given.

"You were loyal to your partner," said King Minos. "On the night the stranger visited me, I wasn't loyal to my family. I made the wrong choice and was cursed and now I have lost my son."

Then Turnbull said, "Remember, we are all in a dream world here. Perhaps I can use the power of my mind to take us all back to the 21st century."

She turned towards King Minos, "But first I need you to promise me that if we get back there will be no more experiments. Tell MI5 to stop working on the secrets of the mind."

"Why?" asked King Minos.

"So that what happened to Roger can never be repeated," Turnbull answered.

"Seems like a great place to end the film," Parker said.

"Let me concentrate," she said, holding her head and closing her eyes.

"Why didn't you do this before?" asked Parker. "You could have done this any time you wanted!"

"Robert, you know very well why I didn't. We hadn't completed our mission," she snapped at him.

There was a flash of light and a rushing sound
in their ears. When they woke up, they were back
in the research labs wearing their 21st-century clothes.
David and Alison Minos were there, as was the
Minotaur. Only now he was back in his human form.
He was Roger once more.

Commander Watson and a crowd of agents were
clapping. Watson went up to Turnbull.

"Welcome back, Laura. You have done an incredible
thing," he said. "You have travelled through time
to rescue our greatest scientist!"

"Thank you, sir," she said.

"And welcome back, David, Roger and Alison.
We're glad that you are back to work on all your
wonderful experiments in the lab," laughed Watson.

"Here, here," said the other Secret Service
commanders.

41

CHAPTER FIVE

Later that day, Agent Turnbull went into her partner's office. As usual she found him sitting at his computer screen.

"Do you think David Minos will keep his promise to me?" she asked.

"It doesn't really matter," Parker replied. "Because *you* are the important one now, Laura. You're the one with the implant in your brain."

"What?" she cried.

"I thought the commander had told you everything," he replied.

She shook her head. "He told me that I had psychic powers. He said that they were thanks to my incredibly evolved lower brain."

Parker got up from his computer. He sat down next to Agent Turnbull and put his arm around her shoulder.

"Laura, when you had that operation on your broken foot a year ago, something strange happened at the same time. I saw an X-ray of your head and saw a small metal object inside it," he explained.

"I think they are investigating your brain. They want to know what it can do and the implant is like a camera. They will already have seen our adventures in Crete on the big screen. They will already know what David Minos promised, but they won't care. His work is history, Laura. Your powers are the future!"

Laura was silent. She was finding it hard to believe what Parker had said to her. "What will become of me?" she sobbed.

"I'll look out for you, Laura. You're a special person to me," Parker said in a low voice. "You're more than just my partner!"

She smiled, even though she was still frightened. "Thank you, Robert. I know I can always trust you," she said. She squeezed his hand and kissed him on the cheek. Who knew what the future had in store?

GLOSSARY OF TERMS

blacked out lost consciousness

Crete an island in the Mediterranean

Greek myths famous stories set in Ancient Greece about gods and heroes

in safe hands in no danger

let sleeping dogs lie to avoid stirring up trouble

lower brain the part of the brain that controls dreams

MI5 government department responsible for national security

Minotaur a mythical creature which was a bull-headed man kept in a labyrinth in Ancient Crete

psychic powers powers of the mind

script the text of a film

Secret Service Government Intelligence Department

3D three dimensional

to have it in for to bear a grudge against

QUIZ

1 Why did Agent Turnbull go to see the doctor?

2 What had Agent Parker seen on the X-ray of Agent Turnbull's skull?

3 What special powers does Agent Turnbull have?

4 In what country was the 3D film in Agent Turnbull's brain set?

5 How many people are in the Minos family? Can you name them?

6 What job did David Minos have?

7 What lived in the maze of tunnels under the palace?

8 What did the stranger show Agent Parker?

9 What did the Minotaur give Agent Turnbull to eat?

10 How did they get back to the 21st century?

ABOUT THE AUTHOR

Paul Blum has taught for over 20 years in London inner-city schools.

I wrote The Extraordinary Files for my pupils so they've been tested by some fierce critics (you!). That's why I know you'll enjoy reading them.

I've made the stories edgy in terms of character and content and I've written them using the kind of fast-paced dialogue you'll recognise from television soaps. I hope you'll find The Extraordinary Files an interesting and easy-to-read collection of stories.

ANSWERS TO QUIZ

1 She was having headaches and strange dream‹

2 A metal implant

3 She has psychic powers

4 Ancient Crete

5 Three: David, Alison and Roger

6 He was the best scientist in MI5

7 The Minotaur

8 A mirror with two futures

9 A pile of bones

10 Agent Turnbull used the power of her mind
    to bring them back